Many years ago there lived a young Jim Hawkins. Jim's father owned an ..... One day, a sailor named Billy Bones came to lodge at his father's inn. The man had a long scar across his face and carried a sea chest with him.

Billy Bones was reserved by nature. He paid Jim four pence a month to keep a lookout for a sailor with one leg. Days passed but no one paid a visit to Billy Bones, until one evening, a mysterious man called Black Dog visited him. Billy Bones was troubled to see him. Soon after the mysterious man left, he fell ill.

A few days later, a blind man named Blind Pew, visited Billy and left the inn after giving him a note bearing a 'black spot'. Billy Bones told Jim, "A black spot means that my old shipmates are coming, they will surely kill me." Billy Bones was so frightened that the next morning he died of a stroke. Without wasting time, Jim told his mother about Billy Bones' mysterious visitors.

Jim's mother quickly took him and went to the village to seek help. Nobody agreed to help them, out of fear. They returned to the inn and forcefully opened Billy Bones' chest. They found a sealed bundle of papers and a pouch filled with gold coins. Jim kept the papers safely and took some money which Billy Bones owed them.

Suddenly, Jim heard the sound of approaching footsteps. He looked out of the window and saw the blind man returning with few more men. "We must escape from here," he told his mother. Without losing a moment, they escaped through the back door, while the blind man kept knocking at the front door.

Jim asked his mother to hide in a safe place and without wasting a moment, he went to meet Dr. Livesey and Squire Trelawney. No sooner had Dr. Livesey opened the sealed packet than he exclaimed, "It's a map to Captain Flint's treasure! We must find it!"

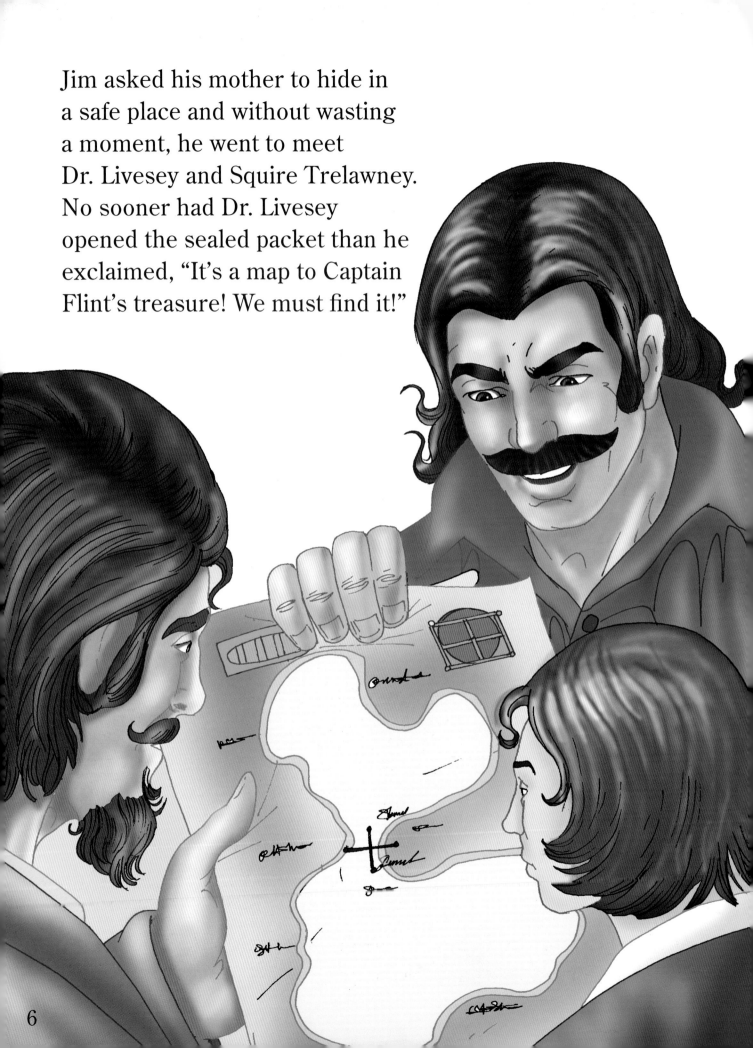

Within days, all preparations were made for the journey
to Bristol. Once there, the Squire introduced Jim to a man
called Long John Silver who had only one leg. He seemed to
be a good tempered fellow. Soon, they met the entire crew
and set sail for the island where the treasure was hidden, on
the ship named, Hispaniola.

One evening, Jim went to the area where barrels filled with food were kept. He found one barrel with only one apple at the bottom. He got into the barrel and sat there quietly, when he overheard Long John Silver and another crew member Israel Hands, planning to kill the captain after the treasure was found. Jim was very frightened. After some time, when he managed to escape from the barrel, he informed the Squire about it. They both took some crew members into confidence. By then, the Hispaniola reached the island.

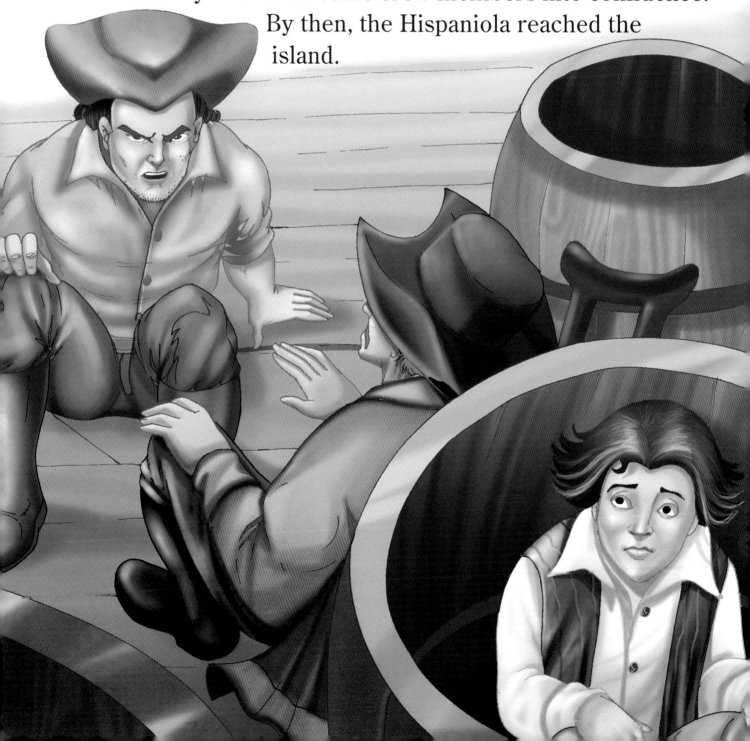

The Captain told the sailors to go to the shore for a while. Jim, too, decided to go with them and slipped into one of the boats. Once he stepped on the island, he ran into the woods where he came across a strange wild looking man. Jim was very frightened to see him.

The man introduced himself as Ben Gunn. He told Jim that he was once a part of Captain Flint's crew. He was abandoned on the island three years back and knew where the treasure was hidden. Meanwhile, Squire, Dr. Livesey and their trusted crew members had also reached the island.

They were hiding in a log house with a Union Jack flying on top, when Jim found them. "We had to leave the ship. The pirates attacked us and seized the ship," said Dr. Livesey. Then, Squire Trelawney suggested that they all must keep a lookout for the pirates. Jim told them about his meeting with Ben Gunn.

The next morning, Jim decided to board the ship. As soon as he boarded the ship, he saw two pirates. One of them was dead and the other was badly wounded. Jim managed to trick him and forced him to take the ship to the other side of the island.

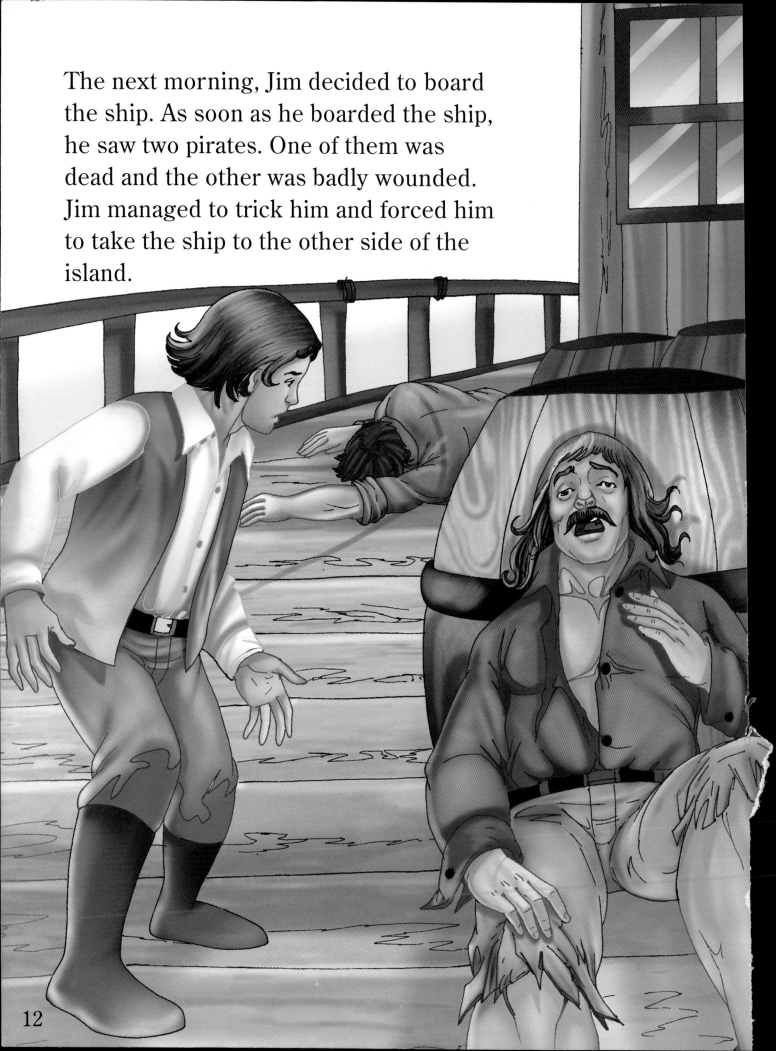

Before returning to the log house, Jim killed the pirate. When he reached there, he found that John Silver and the pirates had taken possession of the log house and the map to the treasure. Jim was worried by this sudden change of events.

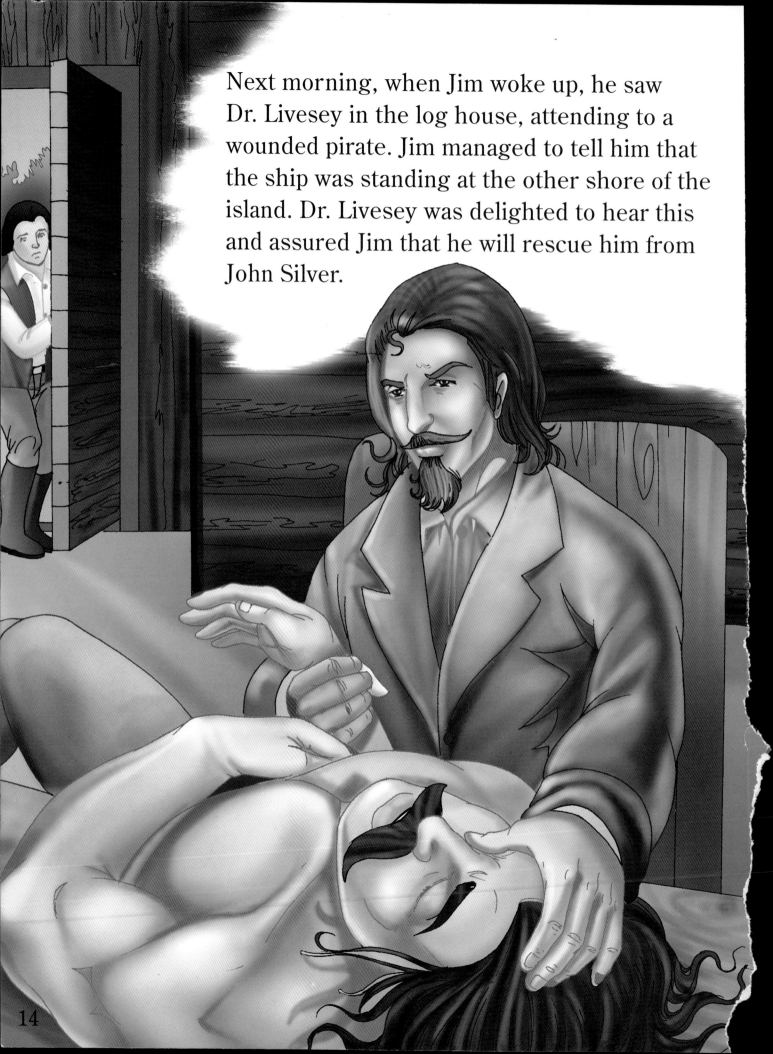

Next morning, when Jim woke up, he saw Dr. Livesey in the log house, attending to a wounded pirate. Jim managed to tell him that the ship was standing at the other shore of the island. Dr. Livesey was delighted to hear this and assured Jim that he will rescue him from John Silver.

After the doctor left, John Silver decided to go in search of the treasure. They followed the pointers on the map and reached the spot where the treasure was supposed to be hidden, but the treasure was missing. The pirates realised that John Silver had cheated them and tried to kill him.

Dr. Livesey and the Squire stopped them and took them to Ben Gunn's cave, where the treasure was safely hidden. The next day, they all set sail for home. They anchored midway at a port and found that John Silver had taken a few gold coins and was missing. Without bothering about him, they headed for home and lived happily ever after.